Dear Parent:
Your child's love of reading starts here!

Every child learns to read in a different way and at his or her own speed. Some go back and forth between reading levels and read favorite books again and again. Others read through each level in order. You can help your young reader improve and become more confident by encouraging his or her own interests and abilities. From books your child reads with you to the first books he or she reads alone, there are I Can Read Books for every stage of reading:

SHARED READING
Basic language, word repetition, and whimsical illustrations, ideal for sharing with your emergent reader

BEGINNING READING
Short sentences, familiar words, and simple concepts for children eager to read on their own

READING WITH HELP
Engaging stories, longer sentences, and language play for developing readers

READING ALONE
Complex plots, challenging vocabulary, and high-interest topics for the independent reader

ADVANCED READING
Short paragraphs, chapters, and exciting themes for the perfect bridge to chapter books

I Can Read Books have introduced children to the joy of reading since 1957. Featuring award-winning authors and illustrators and a fabulous cast of beloved characters, I Can Read Books set the standard for beginning readers.

A lifetime of discovery begins with the magical words **"I Can Read!"**

Visit www.icanread.com for information
on enriching your child's reading experience.

HarperCollins®, ✷®, and I Can Read Book® are trademarks of HarperCollins Publishers.

Transformers Animated: The Decepticons Invade! Copyright © 2008 Hasbro. All Rights Reserved. Printed in the United States of America. No part of this book may be used or reproduced in any manner whatsoever without written permission except in the case of brief quotations embodied in critical articles and reviews. For information address HarperCollins Children's Books, a division of HarperCollins Publishers, 1350 Avenue of the Americas, New York, NY 10019.
www.harpercollinschildrens.com

Library of Congress catalog card number: 2008923458
ISBN 978-0-06-088810-7

1 2 3 4 5 6 7 8 9 10

❖

First Edition

I Can Read!

READING
2
WITH HELP

TRANS FORMERS ANIMATED

THE DECEPTICONS INVADE!

Adapted by Olivia London
Illustrations by Carlo Lo Raso

Based on the episode *Lost and Found*,
written by Rich Fogel

HarperCollinsPublishers

On a sunny day in Detroit,
Sari was playing street hockey
with her friends the Autobots.
Suddenly, her key began to glow.
Danger was near!

Two fireballs zoomed across the sky
and crashed.

The fireballs were Decepticons
named Lugnut and Blitzwing!
They were looking for their leader.
"Where is Megatron?" Lugnut said.

The Autobots knew the Decepticons were going to cause trouble. The Autobots had to stop them!

"Autobots, roll out!"

ordered their leader, Optimus Prime.

"Looking for us?" Optimus called
to the Decepticons.
Ratchet blocked Decepticon missiles
with his shield.

Lugnut threw a truck at Optimus,
but Optimus sliced it in half!
"I think we got their attention,"
said Optimus.

Lugnut was angry.

He smashed his fist into the ground, making a big explosion.

KABOOM!

The blast knocked down the Autobots.

Then the Decepticons disappeared.

Megatron watched Lugnut and
Blitzwing on a video screen.
He knew this was his chance
to get the AllSpark!

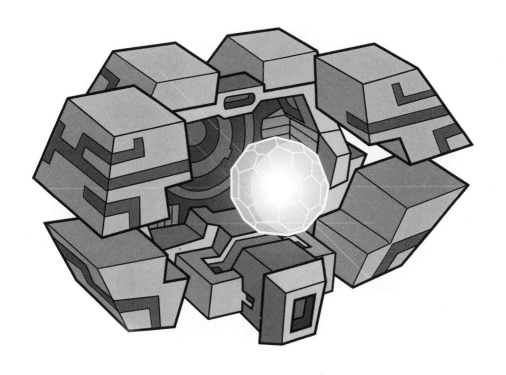

The AllSpark was the source

of all Transformer life.

Megatron needed its power

to defeat the Autobots.

He would make Lugnut and Blitzwing

bring it to him.

The Autobots had survived this battle,
but they knew there would be more.
"We cannot risk causing danger
to this planet," said Optimus.

They would have to take the AllSpark
and leave Earth.

The AllSpark was in
the Autobots' broken ship.
The ship lay at the bottom of a lake.
Only the power from Sari's key
could fix the ship.

But Megatron had a different plan.

He sent Lugnut an image of the key.

"Follow it to the AllSpark," he said.

"Then bring the AllSpark to me!"

At the lake, Ratchet transformed
into an ambulance.

Just then, Sari's key started to glow.

The Decepticons were near!

Lugnut and Blitzwing fired.

"Go to the ship,"

Optimus told Ratchet and Sari.

"We will stay and fight them."

The battle moved underwater.

The Autobots were clever fighters.

Optimus spun his wheels

and made a thick cloud of sand.

Lugnut could not see, and he fired

at Blitzwing by mistake!

While the others were fighting,
Ratchet and Sari found the ship.
Ratchet was so happy to see it.

But Sari was sad.

She did not want her friends to go.

Ratchet knew how Sari felt.

"I will miss you, too," he told her.

"But we must stop the Decepticons!"

Sari knew he was right.

She promised to help fix the ship.

Ratchet told Sari that the ship
had weapons that did not work.

"If we can fix them, we can beat the Decepticons," he said.

They soon came up with a plan.

Ratchet called Optimus
over their radio connection.
"Optimus, draw the Decepticons
to the ship!" he cried.

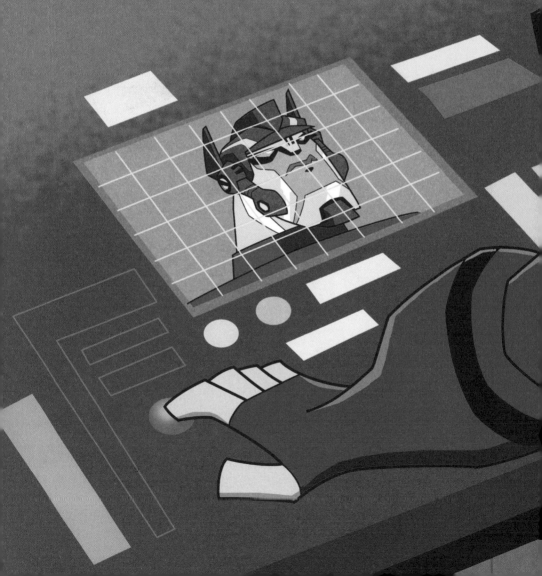

When the Decepticons were close,

Ratchet fired a powerful blast.

It knocked out Lugnut and Blitzwing.

The Autobots had won!

The Autobots and the AllSpark
were safe for now.

"Tomorrow we will finish
fixing your ship," Sari told them.

"No rush," said Ratchet.
"We might stick around
for a very long time!"